Grandma's Library

Story by Krysia Brannon
Art by YoungJu Kim

MOUNTAIN ARBOR
PRESS

This book is dedicated to my mom, Jill Stasiek. She was an incredible mom, grandma, and friend. Whenever I see a Monarch butterfly, I know she is close by.

MOUNTAIN ARBOR
PRESS
Alpharetta, GA

First Edition 2022

ISBN: 978-1-6653-0370-5 – Paperback
ISBN: 978-1-6653-0369-9 – Hardcover

Library of Congress Control Number: 2021923720

Printed in the United States of America   010522

∞ This paper meets the requirements of ANSI/NISO Z39.48–1992 (Permanence of Paper)

Artwork and Design by YoungJu Kim

Tonight, Mom and Dad are having a date night. That means they put on fancy clothes and go out to dinner. I have a date tonight too, with Grandma. I get to put on my cozy pajamas and bring Gigi, my favorite doll!

Going to my Grandma's house is always an adventure! She makes everything so special and fun. Tonight, she said we're going to have a picnic. I know she has been busy all day getting everything ready. I can't wait to see how it looks.

When I get inside, I see a pretty flowered blanket on the floor. Grandma set out her special tea set, so we can be fancy, too. There's even a place for Gigi!

Then I notice a gift bag in the middle of the blanket.
"What's that, Grandma," I ask. "Is it for me?"
"Yes, Elizabeth, it is," she answers. "But first you need
to eat. Then you can open it and see your surprise."

Grandma's eyes twinkle when she says
surprise. I can tell she's up to something,
but I don't know what.
"Fine," I say.
"I guess I can wait."
Then I look up at Grandma
with my best smile.
"But . . . maybe you could give me a hint?"
But Grandma just pats my knee
and points to my dinner.

I eat faster than I ever have before.
Then I look at the bag and ask,
"Can I open it now, Grandma?"
"Go for it!" she says.
I'm so ready to see what's inside the bag
that I quickly pull the tissue out!
A box falls out into my hands.
It has cards, an ink pad, and
a cool looking stamper inside.
"What are these?" I ask,
holding the cards in my hand.

```
                    TITLE
         _____

                   AUTHOR
         _____

LOANED TO: _____

DATE: _____

PHONE №  _____

LOANED TO: _____

DATE: _____

PHONE №  _____

LOANED TO: _____

DATE: _____

PHONE №  _____
```

"Those," Grandma says, "are library cards, for organizing books in a library.

Library cards? Why would I need library cards, I wonder.

Then I see that Grandma's standing up. "Follow me" she says, reaching for my hand.

As we walk upstairs together, Grandma tells me that she has always loved books. She even collected them for a long time. But now, all her books are in a box collecting dust.

"Well, they were in a box," she says.

Grandma opens a door.

"Tada!" she cries.

"Welcome to Grandma's Library!"

I can't believe my eyes.

"Oh, Grandma this is amazing!"

"Books are supposed to be enjoyed,

not left in a box," Grandma says.

"Now come on Elizabeth,

pick out a book for us

to read together."

Grandma's Library

My eyes scan the shelves. There are so many to choose from. Then I see one with a garden on the front. "Beautiful Butterflies," I read.

"Great choice," says Grandma, then we snuggle up together and start reading.

I like butterflies, but I never knew there were so many different kinds of them - and with such funny names. Grandma knows a lot about butterflies. She tells me that Monarch butterflies can travel 3,000 miles in a year and fly above the clouds!

"How do you know so much
about butterflies?" I ask.
"When I was a little girl, I loved going
to the library to pick out books. One of
my favorites was all about butterflies.
My mom made the prettiest paper
butterflies to hang in my room.
I felt like I was in a garden."

I jump up
and
start dancing
around with my arms out,
pretending I'm a butterfly!
"I bet your room was so pretty
with all those butterflies.
I wish I could have seen them," I say.
Grandma smiles and says,
"You know, I may still have them somewhere.
I'll be right back!"

Grandma comes back a few minutes later holding a small, wooden box. Inside are the most beautiful butterflies I have ever seen. "These must have taken so much time for your mom to make," I say, admiring them. "She put a lot of time and love into making them," Grandma says, spreading them out on the floor.

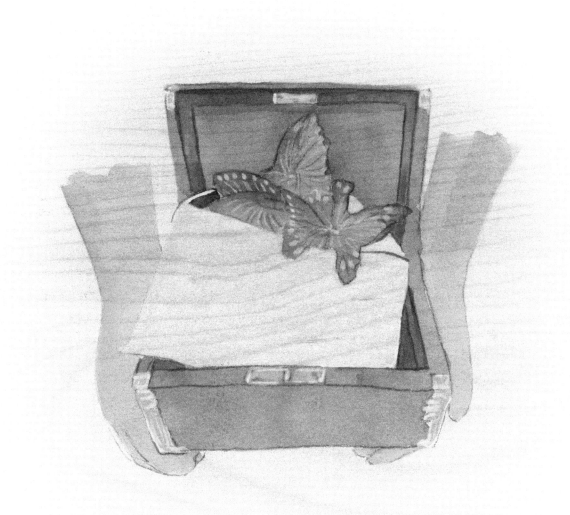

I gently pick one up and make it glide through the air above my head.

"I wish I had butterflies like these to hang in my room," I say.

Grandma smiles. "Next time we have a special date, we will make some together.

"Do you promise?" I ask.

Grandma nods and gives me a hug. Wrapped in her arms,

I smile a big smile. I know I'll get my butterflies.

My grandma always keeps her promises.

We go back downstairs

and Grandma writes

the name of the book

we read on a library card.

I stamp today's date.

"Our first library

book Elizabeth."

She says with

a proud smile.

Suddenly, I hear a knock at the door. It's my parents.

"Can you go on another date tomorrow night?" I ask as soon as I see them.

Mom laughs. "So soon? Why?"

"Because," I say. "Grandma and I have plans!"

A library card is the start of a lifelong adventure.

- Lilian Jackson Brown

How to Create Your Own Library

1. Organize books on a shelf or in baskets.

2. Create a cozy space for reading.

3. Buy or make your own library cards.

4. Enjoy sharing books with someone you love!

Meet the Author

I have been a teacher for twenty years and love reading books to my students. My daughter Elizabeth had a special relationship with my mom. They shared books, conversations, and fun activities together.

Elizabeth is now teaching First Grade and sharing her love of books. I know her Grandma is looking down from heaven and smiling.

Grandma and Elizabeth

Picnic at Grandmas

CPSIA information can be obtained
at www.ICGtesting.com
Printed in the USA
LVHW070125160222
711262LV00006B/124

9 781665 303705